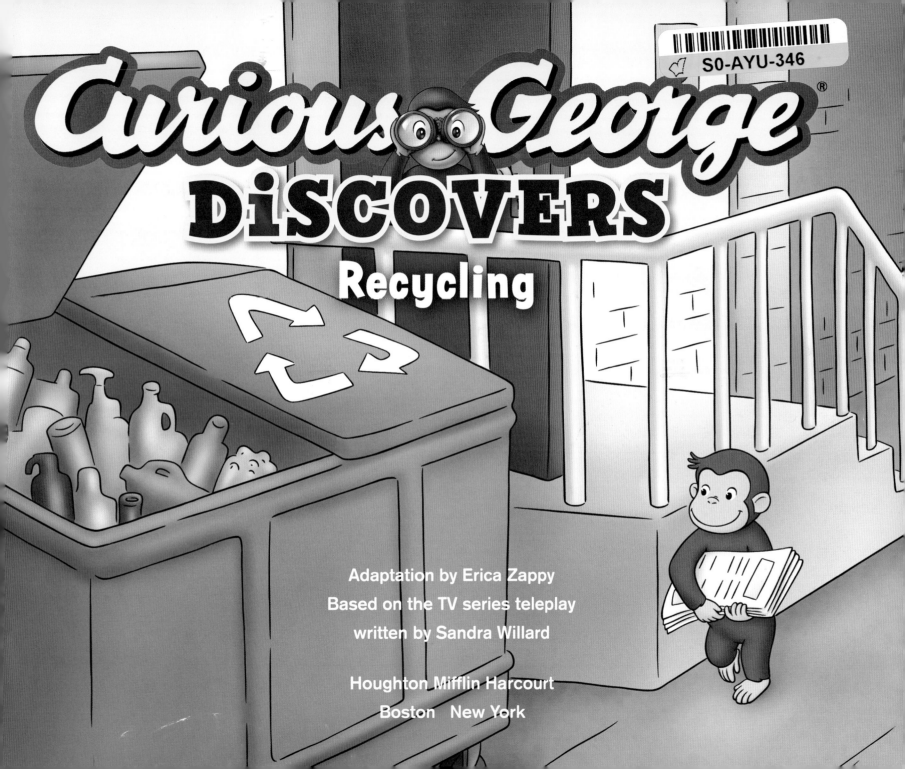

Curious George DISCOVERS

Recycling

Adaptation by Erica Zappy

Based on the TV series teleplay
written by Sandra Willard

Houghton Mifflin Harcourt

Boston   New York

Photographs on cover and pages 7, 12, 15, 17, 23, 30, 31, 32 courtesy of HMH/Carrie Garcia
Photographs on page 9 courtesy of Phelan M. Ebenhack
Photographs on page 16 courtesy of Jody Wissing

Art adaptation by Artful Doodlers Ltd

For information about permission to reproduce selections from this book, write to trade.permissions@hmhco.com or to Permissions, Houghton Mifflin Harcourt Publishing Company, 3 Park Avenue, 19th Floor, New York, New York 10016.

ISBN: 978-0-544-88035-1 paper over board
ISBN: 978-0-544-88036-8 paperback

www.hmhco.com
Printed in China
SCP 10 9 8 7 6 5 4 3 2 1
4500636417

George was a good little monkey, and always very curious. He was especially curious about protecting our environment and keeping the planet clean. Do you want to learn all about recycling with George?

George had been getting ready to throw away a big bag of trash. As he was about to lift the heavy load into the garbage chute, he heard the doorman shout, "Wait! Are you sure that trash is all trash?"

George didn't know what the doorman could be talking about. The bag was filled with things that George and his friend the man with the yellow hat no longer needed and were ready to throw away.

"We need to separate recyclables from trash," the doorman told George, taking the bag. He grabbed a few of the items and tossed them in some big blue bins labeled with arrows. "Recycling makes our planet a lot neater, George! And on top of that," he said, handing him a flyer, "there's a contest for the city's apartment buildings. The building that collects the most recycling wins!"

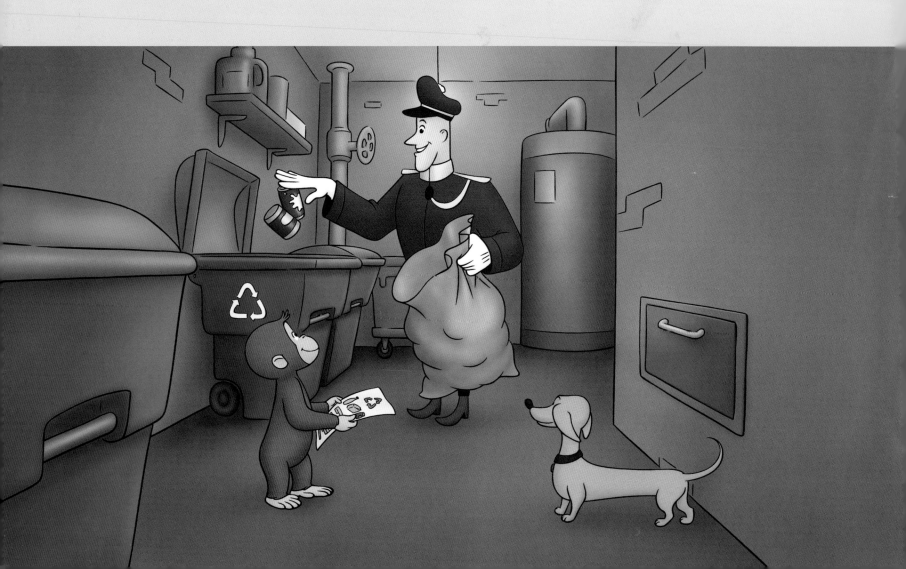

That all sounded great to George . . . except he didn't know what recycling *was*.

George wanted to help recycle, once he figured out how to do it. George showed the flyer to the man.

"Recycling makes old bottles and cans into *new* bottles and cans. Otherwise trash would just pile up all over the planet," said the man with the yellow hat.

This made George very worried. He didn't like thinking about Earth covered in trash.

The man with the yellow hat could tell George was concerned. He had an idea.
"Say, George, would you like to visit the recycling center? Then you can see how this
whole thing works." Just a few minutes ago, George didn't even know what recycling
was. Now he was going to see it in action!

On their way out, they saw the doorman bringing recyclables to the outside bins for the contest. "We're off to an impressive start!" the doorman said.

George and his friend arrived at the recycling center. George saw four big pictures hanging above four big containers. There was a cardboard box, a glass bottle, a tin can, and a plastic jug.

Being a curious monkey, George jumped right into the bin full of glass bottles and jars. Just then a man who worked at the recycling center came over. "My monkey would like to see what recycling is all about," said the man with the yellow hat.

The worker took a glass jar from George's hands, turned it over, and pointed to the bottom. There was something George had never noticed before: three arrows shaped like a triangle. "When you see three arrows like this, it means the item can be recycled," the worker said. "Come with me."

"Once the item gets to the recycling center, the next step is for it to be sorted properly, and then cleaned," the worker explained. George saw lots of jars, bottles, and containers cruising down a conveyor belt. They were going to end up in those big bins he'd seen.

Explore further:
Plastic and glass containers are sent to a recycling center. There they are broken down into smaller bits, melted, and then made into even smaller pieces called granules. Lots of things are made from granules, like more plastic and glass bottles, window frames, and even outdoor furniture.

The worker then showed George a poster. It explained the recycling process. "Recycled glass is broken into small bits, and then melted down. Plastic, too," he said.

en recycled paper could be broken down to make new paper.
eorge could hardly believe this was all possible. There was so
uch to recycle!

Back at the apartment, the competition was heating up and the doorman was worried they were falling behind. Thanks to his visit to the recycling center, George had some good ideas about how he could help recycle. He went upstairs to get started.

In the refrigerator George saw lots of containers he could turn in for the recycling contest. But none of them was empty. The olive jar only had a *few* olives left in it. And the ketchup container was only half full . . . What if George just combined them?

When George finished going through the refrigerator, he moved on to the rest of the apartment building.

He saw big plastic paint buckets with the arrows on the bottom!

He took them.

He saw a grocery delivery just sitting outside an apartment door.

He took the shampoo and juice bottles.

A stack of pizza coupons? That paper could be recycled!

He took the whole pile.

All of these things would help fill his building's recycling bins. George was so happy to be helping and recycling.

While George was collecting these items, the doorman was talking to the doorwoman next door. Her building was competing in the recycling contest as well. "The more people recycle, the better it is for the earth," she said. "And if your building participates in some reuse programs, you'll help the planet even more!"

The doorman didn't know the difference between reusing and recycling. The door-woman explained that reusing simply means using something again. In her building, people leave their magazines in a common area for other people to read. Instead of throwing away moving boxes, they kept them in the basement for other people to use when they needed them.

Did you know . . .

there are lots of ways to help the environment? Have you heard about reduce, reuse, recycle? Reduce means to cut down on the amount of stuff you use every day. For example, instead of using disposable plastic water bottles, you can put your water in a glass or metal bottle to reduce the amount of plastic you use. Reuse means to take the things you've already used and find a way to use them again. Handing down your clothes to friends or younger siblings is a good way to reuse perfectly good pants and shirts. And, of course, you already know lots about recycling by now!

"Hey, I reuse my shopping bags!" said the doorman.

He was already doing it.

When the doorman returned to his recycling bins, they were all filled to the top! The doorwoman was impressed. But the doorman wasn't sure where all this stuff had come from, until . . .

"Someone took my paint pails!"

"My groceries were stolen!"

"Where are our pizza coupons?"

All of their items were in the recycling bins! The doorman was confused. But just then, George came outside carrying another stack of newspapers.

The man with the yellow hat was right behind him. "I think *I* know where the extra recycling came from," the man said, holding his olive jar, which was full of ketchup. "George, you recycle things *after* you use them."

Oops! George had forgotten that part.

After George and the doorman returned all of the extra items, it turned out to be a tie with the doorwoman's building! The two buildings could share the trophy.

George eyed the three big arrows on the front of the trophy.

"That's not recycling, George!" They all laughed.

George would get the hang of recycling soon enough!

RECYCLED CRAFTS

There are lots of things you can make at home with some of the materials you are probably already recycling: plastic bottles and cardboard.

RECYCLED BOTTLE BIRD FEEDER

You will need . . .

- a clean, empty half-gallon milk container or 2-liter soda bottle
- birdseed
- a piece of twine or sturdy string

What to do:

1. Get a grownup to help you cut a hole in the side of your plastic bottle. Make the hole about halfway up the side of the bottle.
2. Fill the bottle with birdseed and then tie a piece of twine around the bottle's lid. You can make this as long or as short as you'd like so that you can hang it from a branch or railing.
3. Then wait for the birds to come check out your feeder! Birds especially love having extra seeds to eat in the wintertime.

RECYCLED ROBOT!

You will need . . .

- an empty cereal box
- a smaller box, such as an empty macaroni and cheese box
- 4 empty toilet paper or paper towel rolls
- glue
- tin foil scraps
- craft supplies, such as glitter, pompoms, bottle caps, sequins, buttons, and feathers

What to do:

1. Have a grownup help you cut one circle on each side and two in the bottom of a cereal box. This is where you can insert your robot's toilet-paper-roll arms and legs.
2. Once your robot has arms and legs, glue your smaller box on top of the cereal box—this will be your robot's head!
3. Glue tin foil over all the cardboard to make your robot look like he's made of metal.
4. Now you are all set to decorate! You can use craft supplies or anything you can find from your recycling to make your robot as shiny and unique as you can imagine.

Did you know...

that nearly 100 percent of a computer can be recycled? Computers are made up of a lot of recyclable material, including plastic, metal, and glass. You may be surprised to know that there are lots of things beyond water bottles and newspapers that can be recycled. Some places recycle batteries, light bulbs, used CDs and DVDs — and yes, even electronics like computers and cell phones. Ask a grownup to help you look online to see what other kinds of things you and your family could be recycling.

REDUCE, REUSE, RECYCLE

How much trash do you throw away? Keep track of everything you throw away for a day: papers, plastics, magazines, cans, even food. You might be surprised!

Once you have your list of all the things you threw out, try to come up with some ways to reduce, reuse, or recycle more of the things you put in the trash each day.

TRASH OR RECYCLING?

Can you figure out what items below are meant to be recycled or reused, and which should be thrown away?